My Ladybug Life

Written & Illustrated by:
Abby Dunford

First Edition
Dunford, Abigail
     My Ladybug Life/Abigail Dunford
     Originally published: Brownsboro, AL.; Just The Box®,
     www.JustTheBox.com
     ISBN: 978-1-4507-5076-9

Layout Design by Mike Dozier, MKADesigns
Printed by Lightning Source, Inc

Dedicated to those who live their dreams.

Good night stars...
Good night moon...
And may you dream of at least six impossible
things before morning...

"Hello! My name is Abby. Now, if you did not say that with a British accent, please return to the beginning and try again. In fact, this entire story is to be read with your British accent.

My story is fiction (big word for not bloody true, or based on facts, so my Dad says) and it all came from my imagination. However, I do have some non-fiction, which means, true facts also...such as how I, as a ladybug protect myself. So my friend, I have written how I would see a day in the life of a ladybug or, "My Ladybug Life"....and I am a ladybug who keeps a journal or a diary. This book is my ladybug diary, albeit but just for a few days. Can you imagine seeing the world as they do? Do they even see and hear like a human?

I hope you have as much fun reading my book as I did writing. I also included on the back page a drawing of ladybugs that you may color as you imagine ladybugs to be colored. My Dad always tells me that we learn most when we can mark on a book, so I like to color so coloring it is. Enjoy.

Cheerio!

Annie, Dad and Abby

In a land far, far away...

No really, in a land far,
fffaaaarrrr, away...

May 23, 2010, 9:00 a.m.

Hi my name is Ladybug Lena (Lele for short).

Anyway, I have this awkward tasting fluid in my body so if a predator wants to eat me I'll squirt it all over its eyes. I'm just kidding. I just squirt it on me so they will leave me alone.

So, I have ran a mile before! Well, I have flown a mile. I can't run exactly....legs to short, feet to small.

I have six friends. Their names are Lindsey, Lachlen, Lenarella, Lohand, Logan and Millie.

10:00 a.m.

I go to Ladybug Elementary.
I am in the third grade.

I eat aphids and plants for lunch every day.

Do you know what an aphid is? It is a ghastly sap sucking little creature that can destroy plants. In Britain they are known as "plant lice".

The good part about being a ladybug is that you don't have to do a lot of chores. I do have to watch out for jars when I fly because some crazy humans will catch me. I also had to play dead today F-O-U-R TIMES!...because a frog, a wasp, a spider, and a dragonfly tried to eat me.

11:00 a.m.

I remember I also have to go play with my friends today! Well, bye for now.

OK, I am here with my friends now. I just heard we are going to play tag! 1, 2, 3…NOT IT! NOT IT! NOT IT!

Sorry, we had to see who was it! Lyndsey is it! She doesn't pay attention to what we say sometimes.

AAAAAAAHHHHHHH…HELP! She's chasing me!!!

Whew! I thought she was going to….

AAAAAAAHHHHHHH….she's chasing me again!!!!!!

12:00 P.M.

I'm here with my friends eating lunch at my house. Yum! I love fried aphids and grilled plants.

Oh, here come the water droplets. I'm ssssssssssssooooooooo thirsty. What!? I have to share a droplet with Lindsey?
Oh come on!..what's a ladybug to do?

"Ok, you can share the water only if I get to have a drink first." GULP, GULP, GULP. "AAAAAHHHHH that was good water."

"Hey! You drank all the water!"

"Oops. Fine, I'll just go get some more water myself and you get none of it Lele."

2:00 P.M.

OMG!

I can't believe Massie and Claire became friends.

Oh you people are listening to my life and how it works again. My apologies.

 OK, right now I'm reading my books so I can get fifty advance reader or A.R. Points. (A. R. is a reading program where you earn points for reading books and at my school, the person with the highest number of points at the end of the year wins a trophy!)

I love to read... ever read "My Little Butterfly"?

Ring, Ring!
Oh, it must be Lindsey calling to apologize.

"Hello... is anybody there...hello."

"Hi, my name is Sam the Spider."

 AAAAAAAHHHHHH!
That is the spider that
tried to eat me!

AAAAAAAAHHHHHHH!!!!!!!!!

"Yes. You are correct. I called to see where
you lived so I can eat you."

"No way, I am not telling you where I live."

"HAHAHAHAHAHAHA that is so funny."

"What is so funny?"

"It's me, Lindsey. I did that so I could take
revenge from this morning."
"Come on Lindsey, you scared me so much I
peed in my pants."

5:00 P.M.

 Today I went to the candy store. I got chocolate covered leaves and licorice aphids. It was so good. I'm eating dinner in three minutes. I'm so full because I ate all that candy.

Oh, I know, I will say, "Mom, I need to use the restroom," and then I'll throw the food away. I am a genius!

"Lele, it is time to eat."

"OK, I'm coming." Here comes my awesome plan. Waaaaahahahahah!

Mother dear, I need to go to the bathroom. May I be excused?"

"You may be excused."

Oh no, how will I get the food off my plate?
Oh, I got it! When they are not looking I will

get the food and go to the bathroom.
OK, they are not looking, I'll get my food now.
I'm flying.
Oh I'm here.
Thump thump thump.
Flush.
My plan worked.

I'm so tired.
"Mom may I please go to bed I am so tired."
"Go ahead honey."

maddie's room
good night, sleep tight.
don't let the bed bugs bite.
if they do bit 'em back,
twice as hard!

9:00 A.M. May 24, 2010
Oh, I am so tired. I just woke up. I want to go to bed and wake up again.

Oh well, today I have music practice. I can't wait! OK, I'm going to sing to you. Here I go.

(The song is sung to tune of "All Star" by Smash Mouth)

Somebody once told me the world was macaroni.
So I took a bite out of a tree. It felt kind of funny.
So I played with a bunny and the bunny started playing with me.

I like it. Do you?

Oh no, I'm not dressed yet and practice starts in two minutes.

AAAAAAAAAAHHHHHHHHHHH!!!!!!!!!!!!!!!
What am I going to do?
"Mom, may I have some breakfast?"

I'm really going to the movies with my friends today.

Thanks mom."
What!...She only gave me fried plants. Oh my gosh!

11:00 A.M.

That movie was so good.
It was called...The Spy Next Door.
My mom is probably worried sick because I said
I would be back in an hour.

HURRY!
HURRY!
HURRY!

Oh, come on.
I would have called my mom,
but I don't have a cell phone.
Uh oh.

"You guys? You guys where are
you?"

Great! I'm stranded at a parking lot. I'll fly
then. Oh, here comes a taxi. "Taxi."
I'm having the worst day of
my life.

First I get stranded at a
parking lot, and then I miss a
decent taxi. I'm flying.

2:00 P.M.

My little sister is having a birthday party tonight. She's turning six. I don't really think her friends are very cool so I am going to bed at five o'clock. Really?

One of her friends is already here.
"Hi Lele."
Oh great, my least favorite friend of Amanda's is here first.

Ding dong.
Here comes another of Amanda's friends.
A few minutes later. Oh my gosh. Everyone is here already.

"Let's play pin the wing on Lele." "

AAAAAAAAAAAAHHHHHHHHHHHHH!!!!!!!

Help! They are trying to poke me with a needle. Mom make them stop!

"Let's play another game."

"What should we play Lele?"
"Maybe we could have a water balloon fight."
"Yeah, that is a great idea.
Let's get our bathing suits on."
Splash! Splash! Splash!
"I...I...I am sssssoooo cold."

5:00 P.M.
Ok, I am getting in my pajamas.

Oh, I am so comfortable in my bed.
The kids are watching a movie. So I can go to bed.
Sorry, but I am so tired.

I wish they could turn the volume down just a little bit more.
"You guys please turn the volume down."

"Ok Lele we will."
"Thanks, that is much better."

I have to fall asleep right now. But, the volume is still a little bit loud...

"Turn the volume down just a little bit more please."

"Lele, if we turn it down any more we won't be able to hear it."

Never mind I'll just go to sleep...tomorrow is another day

ZZZZZZ....zzzzzz.....

Your ladybugs to color...Abby D.

CPSIA information can be obtained at www.ICGtesting.com
Printed in the USA
BVIW120534180419
545792BV00014B/79